Mr Bear's Holiday

Debi Gliori

ORCHARD BOOKS

with lots of love
to Caroline and Dave
and Alice and Oliver and Holly~
crossing continents
and turning their lives
into an adventure

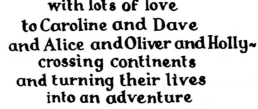

ORCHARD BOOKS
96 Leonard Street, London EC2A 4XD
Orchard Books Australia
14 Mars Road, Lane Cove, NSW 2066
First published in Great Britain 2000
© Debi Gliori 2000
ISBN 1 84121 195 8
The right of Debi Gliori to be identified as the author and the
illustrator of this work has been asserted by her in accordance
with the Copyright, Designs and Patents Act, 1988.
A CIP catalogue record for this book is available from the British Library.
10 9 8 7 6 5 4 3 2 1
Printed in Hong Kong/China

"Look Small, a postcard's
come for you," said Mrs Bear.
"Lucky Grizzle-Bears,
they're on holiday."

"Can we go on holiday?" said Small Bear. "On a plane?
Or a rocket or a ship or a train?"

"A holiday," said Mr Bear, emerging from behind his paper.
"That's a good idea. How about in a tent?"

"What's a tent?" asked Small Bear.

"Wait and see," said Mrs Bear.
"Let's have breakfast first."

After breakfast,
they all helped to get ready.
Mr Bear found the tent.
Small Bear found the sleeping bags.
Baby Bear found the maps.

Mrs Bear organised the food, suncream, candles and sunglasses, hats, cups, forks, knives, spoons, matches, elastoplasts and four honey sandwiches, just in case.

By lunchtime they were ready.

"I love holidays," said Small Bear, as they set off. "Where are we going?"

"Wait and see," said Mr Bear staggering under the weight of the rucksack. "It's an adventure."

It was a very long adventure.
First, they stopped to change Baby Bear's nappy.

"Are we there yet?" said Small Bear.
"Not yet," said Mr Bear.

A little later they stopped to eat their sandwiches.
"When are we going to be there?" said Small Bear.
"Soon," said Mr Bear. "Be patient."

A long time later, they stopped to look at the map.
"Do you know where we're going?" said Small Bear.
"Sort of," said Mr Bear. "Not far now,"
he added hopefully.

The sun was beginning to slip behind the trees when Mr Bear finally stopped.

"Here we are," he said, dropping the rucksack with a groan.

Small Bear looked around.

"Is this a holiday?" she said suspiciously.

"NO!" snapped Mr Bear.
"It's an ADVENTURE!"

Small Bear's bottom lip began to quiver.
"Let's go and find some wood for the fire,"
said Mrs Bear, "and leave Dad and Baby Bear
to put up the tent."

Mrs Bear and Small Bear headed for the woods.
Watched by Baby Bear, Mr Bear unrolled the tent.
Several hundred moths flew out.
Baby Bear clapped her paws in delight.
"Oh dear," said Mr Bear. "Poor *tent*."

Baby Bear watched in silent wonder as Mr Bear struggled heroically with the holey tent. Ropes snapped and poles bent, but eventually Mr Bear succeeded in putting the tent up.

"There," he said. "Just the right size for the four of us."

"Look who I found," said Small Bear,
running back. "Can Flora stay too?"
"We met all her family in the woods,"
sighed Mrs Bear. "Mrs Rabbit-Bunn would've
liked them all to come along..."

The first stars were just appearing in the sky as the Bear family and their guest sat down to supper.

"Sorry it's a bit burnt," said Mrs Bear.

"It's delicious," said Mr Bear. "This is what holidays are about: firelight, starlight and supper in the open air…"

A large cloud blotted out the stars, and from nowhere a chill wind began to blow. The bears huddled round the fire. Flora climbed onto Small Bear's lap.

Mr Bear rummaged in the rucksack.

"Oh dear," he said.

"What's the matter?" said Mrs Bear.

"I forgot to pack the sleeping bags," said Mr Bear.

Baby Bear began to cry. Small Bear's bottom lip wobbled dangerously.

"Never *mind*," muttered Mrs Bear, glaring at Mr Bear, "we'll just huddle together in our nice warm tent."

It wasn't much warmer in the nice warm tent.

"Look," said Small Bear. "I can see the stars through the roof."

"Yes," said Mrs Bear grimly. "And you can feel the wind too."

"What's *that?*" said Mr Bear.
"What?" said Mrs Bear.
"That snorting sound,"
whispered Mr Bear.
"Outside, listen…"
The bears fell silent.
Flora's ears twitched.

"Look," said Mrs Bear in a trembly whisper.
"There, on the wall."
"AAARGH!" screamed Mr Bear.
"It's a MONSTER!" wailed Small Bear.
"MooOOO," said the monster.

Mr Bear stuck his head out of the tent to investigate.
"Oh DEAR," he said.
"MooOO SNORT," said the monster,
        leaning on the tent.

"Quick! Let's go!" yelled Mr Bear, stuffing
the little bears into the rucksack and pulling
Mrs Bear and Flora after him.
They sprinted away from the
tent, just as it collapsed under
the weight of a curious cow.

The bears walked home by moonlight.
Just as they had returned Flora to her burrow,
a shadow swooped down from the treetops.
The Bear Family yelped.

"It's only me," said Mr Hoot-Toowit.
"You're all so *jumpy* – I think you need a holiday."

"We've only just *had* a holiday," said Small Bear.

"Did you have a nice time?" said Mr Hoot-Toowit.

The Bears smiled a secret smile.
"Well," laughed Mr Bear, "I think we all need
another holiday to recover from our holiday."